By Bonnie Brooke
Illustrated by David Prebenna

Published by Bendon Publishing International, Inc. All rights reserved.
Printed in Haining, Zhejiang, China.

The BENDON name is a trademark of Bendon Publishing International, Inc.
Ashland, Ohio 44805. 1-888-5-BENDON. bendonpub.com
 81319-TG F 0214

Time to get up, Elmo!
Up, up, up!

The big pup is up.
The pup smells a cupcake.
Yum!

Cookie Monster!
Do not eat up
all the cupcakes!

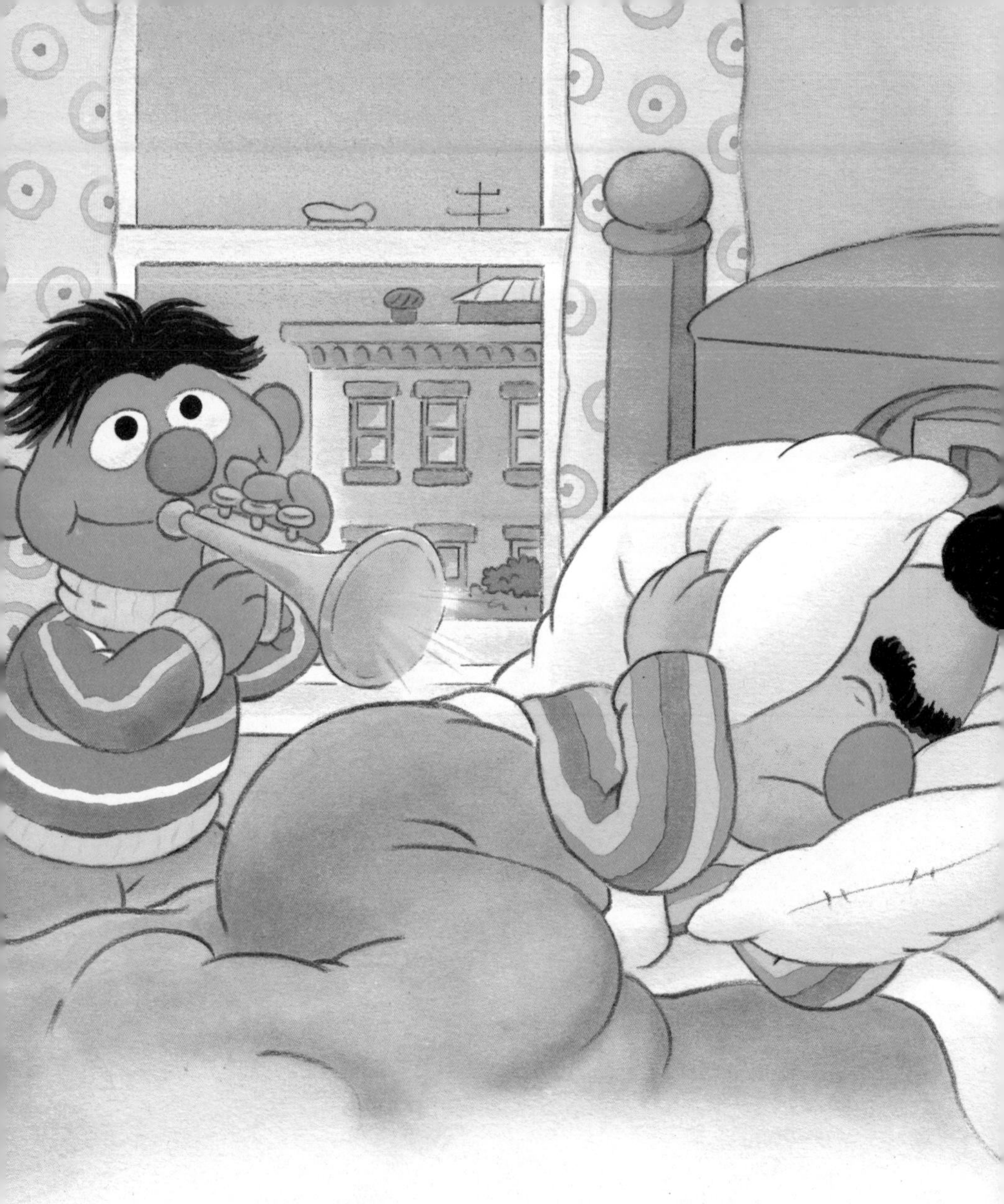

Ernie is up,
but Bert is not.
Toot-toot-TOOT!
"Stop, Ernie! I give up."

Oh, look!
The baby is up.
The dolly is down.
Down, down, down.

Farmer Grover calls
to six sleepy cows.

“Wake up, cows!
Time for me to milk!”

Oscar pops up.
Bang! Clang! Scram!

Pick up the papers.
One! Two! Three!

Get up, Benny.
The bags must go
up, up, up!

La-la-la!
It is time to wash up!
Scrub-a-dub-dub!

Brush up!
Up and down.

(Not too much!
Do not use it up.)

Bert is up.
What will he put on?
He cannot make up his mind.

Bam! Bam! Bam!

Herry runs up
the street.

All the monsters are up!
All the monsters are out!

Where is Elmo?
Is Elmo up?

Now the monsters are in.
It is time to eat up.

Where is Elmo?
Is Elmo up?

The sun is up.
The birds are up.
And now Elmo is up.
Up, up, up!